LITTLE MANILLA
AND
THE SECRET
OF SUCCESS

WRITTEN BY: SOOZ OLSON &
ROCHELLE SCHELLINGER

ILLUSTRATED BY: SOOZ OLSON

This Book is dedicated to:

Chelsea and Grace
Kash and Atlas

To order additional copies of this book, contact:
Xlibris
844-714-8691
www.Xlibris.com
Orders@Xlibris.com

ISBN: 978-1-6698-2711-5 (sc)
ISBN: 978-1-6698-2712-2 (e)

Print information available on the last page

Rev. date: 08/16/2022

As you read this book,

Think about how each animal figures out what it takes to be **successful**.

Think about <u>YOUR</u> dreams and goals
and what <u>YOU</u> need to do
to be **successful**.

You dear soul are beautiful and unique,

here to create the goals that you seek.

This is the story of the secret of success.

A young chinchilla named Little Manilla
was always playing around,
    rolling in dust balls,
    and taking naps.

She didn't take life seriously.

Momma & Poppa Chinchilla worried about Little Manilla.

- How will she live by herself?
- How will she get her own food?
- How will she make friends?
- How will she be successful?

Momma Chinchilla said,
"Little Manilla, you will have to learn the secret of success!"

So Little Manilla set out to find out about success.

Soon Little Manilla saw a bird upon the road.
Little Manilla said, "Hi, Gunner, the road runner.
Can you tell me the secret of success?"

"Chirp, Chirp!" said Gunner.
"Don't be afraid to get started.
Decide on each goal and dream.
Start with what makes your heart beam."

"Chirp, Chirp!" said Gunner;
and off ran Gunner, the road runner."

Little Manilla didn't know what to think about that.
"Hmmmm," so she decided to ask someone else.

Soon Little Manilla saw another animal in the desert.
Little Manilla said, "Hi Chillo, the armadillo.
Can you tell me the secret of success?"

"Scratch, scratch!" said Chillo.
"When attacked or when you fall,
protect yourself, curl into a ball."

"Scratch, scratch!" said Chillo;
and off waddled Chillo, the armadillo."

Little Manilla didn't know what to think about that.
"Hmmmm," so she decided to ask someone else.

Soon Little Manilla saw another animal on her path.
Little Manilla said, "Hi Morris, the tortoise.
Can you tell me the secret of success?"

"Chomp, chomp, hiss, hiss!" said Morris, as he chewed
on cactus.
"Success is going at a steady pace. Think of it like a race.
At times you move fast and other times you go at a
slower pace."

"Chomp, chomp, hiss, hiss!" said Morris;
and off stepped Morris, the tortoise."

Little Manilla didn't know what to think about that.
"Hmmmm," so she decided to ask someone else.

Soon Little Manilla saw another animal in a pond.
Little Manilla said, "Hi Trish, the fish.
Can you tell me the secret of success?"

"Glub, glub!" said Trish, the fish.
"In your pond you swim around.
Stay active, get out of your nook.
and don't get distracted with the silver hook!"

"Glub, glub!" said Trish;
and off swam Trish, the fish.

Little Manilla didn't know what to think about that
and didn't like swimming.
Hmmmm, so she decided to ask someone else.

Soon Little Manilla saw other animals in the meadow.
Little Manilla said, "Hi Toni, the pony.
Can you tell me the secret of success?"

"Whinny, whinny, neigh, neigh!" said Toni.
"Goals are nothing without actions!
Positive goals will yield super reactions!
A supportive herd may light the way.
They may help you find the hay."

"Whinny, whinny, neigh, neigh!" said Toni;
and off trotted Toni, the pony.

Little Manilla didn't know what to think about that,
"Hmmmm," so she decided to ask someone else.

Soon Little Manilla saw another animal in the grass.
Little Manilla said, "Hi, Cabbot, the jack rabbit.
Can you tell me the secret of success?"

"Twitch the nose, hop the lop!" said Cabbot.
"Beware of negative events!
There are bumps and valleys along the way.
Don't worry, keep on going without delay."

"Twitch the nose, hop the lop!" said Cabbot;
and off hopped Cabbot, the jack rabbit.

Little Manilla didn't know what to think about that.
"Hmmmm," so she decided to ask someone else.

Soon Little Manilla saw another animal upon the plateau.
Little Manilla said, "Hi, Bodee, the coyote.
Can you tell me the secret of success?"

"Yip, yip, yip, howl!" said Bodee.
"Focus on what you really want.
Think about it. Concentrate.
Keep your eyes on the prize, then success will arise."

"Yip, yip, yip, howl!" said Bodee;
and off scampered Bodee, the coyote.

Little Manilla didn't know what to think about that,
"Hmmmm," so she decided to ask someone else.

Soon Little Manilla saw another animal on the plains.
Little Manilla said, "Hi Jizelle, the gazelle."
Can you tell me the secret of success?"

"Snort, snort!" said Jizelle, as she munched on grass.
"Keep alert, and nourish!
Before you leap and bound,
cherish the treasures you have found."

"Snort, snort!" said Jizelle;
and off bounded, Jizelle, the gazelle.

Little Manilla didn't know what to think about that,
"Hmmm," so she decided to ask someone else.

Soon Little Manilla saw another bird in the trees.
Little Manilla said, "Hi, Rawl, the owl.
Can you tell me the secret of success?"

"Whoo, whoo, ha-whoo!" said Rawl.
"You need to visualize with your eyes.
Do the right thing. Make your heart sing.
Don't sit on the shelf. Be true to yourself."

"Whoo, whoo, ha-whoo!" said Rawl;
and off flew Rawl, the owl.

Little Manilla had a lot to think about! "Hmmmm,"

And so my dear. . . . .

The secret to your success
              is to always do your best.
Let go of your doubt;
              let go of your fear.
Do the action required
              to make it all clear!

Believe in yourself!

You, dear soul, are beautiful and unique,
here to create the dreams that you seek.

When you believe in your dreams,
they can carry you to the stars.
May the dreams of your heart come to be,
and open up a world where your spirit can run free.

**Celebrate the adventurous spirit that makes <u>YOU,</u>
who <u>YOU</u> are!**

Shoot for the Moon and Stars!

Now Little Manilla knew the "Secret of Success".

Get started – decide on goals.
Protect yourself.
Keep going at a steady pace.
Stay active, don't get distracted.
Positive goals will yield super reactions.
Beware of what is negative – don't worry.
Focus – concentrate! Keep your eyes on the prize.
Keep alert & cherish treasures found.
Do the right thing. Make your heart sing.
Always do your best.

But most of all,
     believe in yourself and believe in your dreams!

Printed in the United States
by Baker & Taylor Publisher Services